Bad Boys
Get
Cookie!

by Margie Palatini ◆ illustrated by Henry Cole

KATHERINE TEGEN BOOKS
An Imprint of HarperCollins *Publishers*

Also by Margie Palatini and Henry Cole

Bad Boys

Bad Boys Get Cookie!
Text copyright © 2006 by Margie Palatini
Illustrations copyright © 2006 by Henry Cole
Manufactured in China.

Library of Congress Cataloging-in-Publication Data
Palatini, Margie.
    Bad boys get cookie! / by Margie Palatini ; illustrated by Henry Cole. — 1st ed.
        p.   cm.
    Summary: Wolves Willy and Wally try to satisfy a sweet-tooth craving by dressing up as private eyes and
chasing down a runaway cookie.
    ISBN-10: 0-06-074436-7 (trade bdg.) — ISBN-13: 978-0-06-074436-6 (trade bdg.)
    ISBN-10: 0-06-074437-5 (lib. bdg.) — ISBN-13: 978-0-06-074437-3 (lib. bdg.)
    [1. Cookies—Fiction. 2. Wolves—Fiction.] I. Cole, Henry, date, ill. II. Title.
PZ7.P1755Bc 2006
[E]—dc22   2005018102

Typography by Elynn Cohen   1 2 3 4 5 6 7 8 9 10   ❖   First Edition

For my bad boy

−M.P.

Those bad boys, Willy and Wally Wolf,
had two big bad sweet tooths.
Bad. Bad. Really, really bad.

"Please toss me another caramel, dear pal," said Willy to Wally.

"I believe I could go for a couple of bonbons myself," said Wally to Willy, popping two sugary morsels into his mouth.

But mere candy was not enough to stop two big bad sweet tooths of two big bad wolves. Oh, heavens no!

Those bad boys wanted something decidedly more filling.

A piece of chocolate cake? A slice of pecan pie?

A bit of brownie?

"Help! Help! Someone get my cookie!"

Willy's ears perked. Wally's eyes twinkled. They both giggled and drooled. Brain ditto!

"We can get Cookie."

The boys grabbed their fedoras, made a quick exit, and dashed lickety-split to the worried baker.

The two quickly introduced themselves as private eyes Willis and Wallace from the well-known detective agency of Dewey-Ketchum and Howe.

"But can you get my cookie?" asked the fretting Mr. Baker.

"Sir, that's our specialty," said Willy with a smooth smile.

"Just give us a description of the cookie in question and we'll be right on the case," added Wally, notepad in hand and pencil pointed.

"Well," began the baker, "he's about this high. Thin. Lightly browned. Full of sugar and spice. Dark raisin eyes. Round currant mouth. He's wearing a white-icing jacket with gumdrop buttons. Oh dear, he's just hot out of the oven."

"We know the type," said Wally with a nod.

The baker sighed. "I thought he was such a good cookie. I don't know what's gotten into him. I gave him the best of everything. Butter. Cream. Sugar."

"Don't worry," said Willy. "Detective Wallace and I will sniff him out."

Wally grinned at Willy. Willy grinned at Wally. They both licked their lips.

Yes. Those boys were bad. Bad. Really, really bad.

"There he is now!" cried the baker, pointing toward the hill.

The baker shook his head. "Oh dear. I'm afraid I added too much spice."

"Don't fear, Mr. Baker. We know just how to handle him. Willis and Wallace always get their cookie."

Those bad boys huffed up the hill. Puffed down a dale. And blew through a couple of fields of head-high corn.

But . . . they could not get Cookie.

"Na-na-ni-na-na! Lookee! Lookee! You can't get me. I'm one smart cookie!"

Willy looked at Wally.

Wally looked at Willy.

Brain ditto!

Yes, those bad boys needed a plan! An idea!

A trap!

Oh my, they were clever!

Oh my, they were cunning!

PLAN A

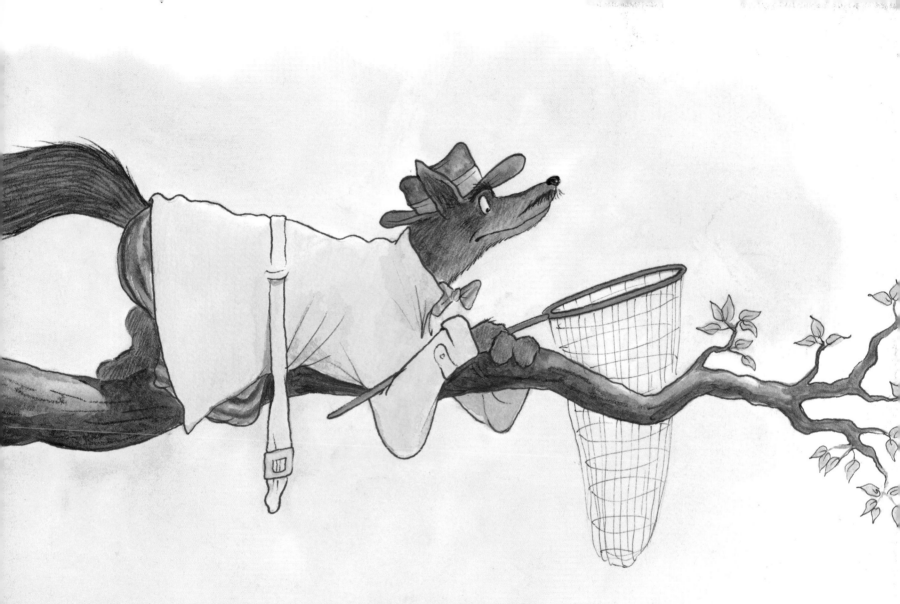

"And bad. Bad. Really, really bad." The two snickered as they climbed out on a limb.

The boys waited. They watched. They inched. Further. Farther. And then . . .

"Get Cookie!" they shouted.

Cr-r-r-RACK!

Ka-BOOM!

"Oh dear," said Willy, seeing stars. "Do you think perhaps we went out a *bit* too far?"

"Na-na-ni-na-na! Lookee! Lookee!

You can't get me. I'm one smart cookie!"

Willy looked at the tangled
Wally. Wally looked at the tangled Willy.

Brain ditto!

Those bad boys needed another plan! Another idea!

A disguise!

Oh my, they were clever! Oh my, they
were cunning!

"And so cute too." They both giggled.

"Oh, woe is me," cried Willy as Cookie pranced into view.

"Woe is me too. Boo-hoo. Boo-hoo." Wally moaned as Cookie came closer. "Oh, brother Hansel. Lookee! Lookee!"

"Yah, sister Gretel," said Willy with a wink. "That is one smart cookie. And he looks so sweet too. Maybe he will help us get back to our mama and papa."

"Lookee. Lookee, little Cookie. We kiddies are lost in the woods," said Wally. "Could you spare a few crumbs so we can find our way out of the forest?"

Cookie looked at Willy.
Cookie looked at Wally.
He came closer. And closer.

So close those bad boys could
almost grab a taste of the sugar
and spice!

"Get Cookie!" they shouted.

"Na-na-ni-na-na! Lookee! Lookee!
You can't get me. I'm one smart cookie!"

Willy looked at the dizzy Wally.

Wally looked at the dizzy Willy.

Brain ditto!

Those bad boys needed another plan. Another idea.

A trick!

"It's a honey," said Wally with a sticky squirt.

"Sweet!" Willy chuckled as he squeezed from behind into the hollow log.

"One slip. One slide. One Cookie!"

From inside the inky darkness, the pair waited. And listened.
And then . . .

They heard a slip. They heard a slide.

They felt a bump!

"I do believe we finally *got* Cookie!" exclaimed Willy.

Wally took a whiff.

"I'm afraid, dear chum, that is not the aroma of sugar and spice."

"Peeeuuew!"

the two squealed, scrambling out from the
log and jumping into the river.

"Na-na-ni-na-na! Lookee! Lookee!
You can't get me. I'm one smart cookie!"

Cookie tossed them each a gumdrop button and waved
good-bye as he floated away on a log.

Willy turned to Wally and grinned.

"I believe that little crumb is not as smart as he thinks he is."

"Yes, indeedy," Wally agreed with a snicker. "But I must say, I've worked up quite an appetite trying to get that one little Cookie."

"I have to agree, old chum," said Willy as his belly grumbled. "Just one little sweet isn't going to cure my sweet tooth or empty tummy now."

Wally offered Willy his arm.

"Well, dear pal, what shall we have for supper?"

"Yoo-hoo! Kiddies! . . . Why don't you help yourselves to something to eat at my house? I've got the oven warming right now."

Willy looked at Wally.

Wally looked at Willy.

Brain ditto!

Ah yes. Oh my. Those boys were bad. Bad. Really, really bad.